Flap Your Wings

Flap Your Wings

by P.D. Eastman

BEGINNER BOOKS

A Division of Random House, Inc.

An egg lay in the path.

A boy came down the path.

He saw the egg.

He looked around.

He saw flamingos and frogs,

and turtles and alligators.

"Whose egg is this?" he called.

But nobody answered.

Then the boy looked up.

He saw an empty nest in a tree.

"Here is an egg without a nest," he said,

"and there is a nest without an egg."

The boy climbed the tree.

He put the egg

in the nest.

Then he went away.

Mr. and Mrs. Bird came home.
They were surprised to find
an egg in their nest.
"That's not **our** egg," said Mrs. Bird.
"Look how big it is!"

"But it is an egg. It's in our nest,"
said Mr. Bird.
"If an egg is in your nest,
you sit on it and keep it warm.
It doesn't matter
whose egg it is."

"All right," said Mrs. Bird.
"But I wonder what kind of bird
will come out of that egg."

They took turns keeping the egg warm.

First Mrs. Bird sat on it.

Then Mr. Bird sat on it.

And sometimes,
because it was so big,
they both sat on it.

One day Mrs. Bird heard
a squeaking noise.
"Help!" she said.
"This egg is squeaking!"

SQUEAK SQUEAK SQUEAK

Mr. Bird came back to the nest.

He listened to the egg.

"The egg is not squeaking," he said.

"It's our baby that is squeaking.

He is ready to come out of the egg."

Mr. and Mrs. Bird waited.

The egg started to crack.

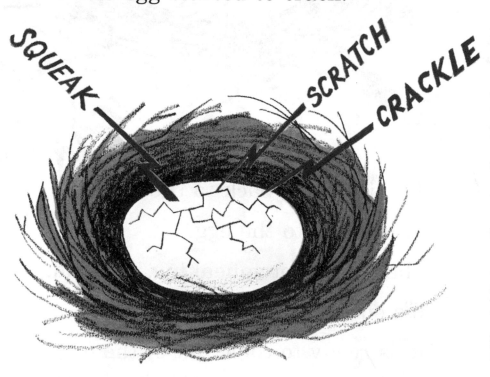

Then it cracked some more.

And there was the baby!

Mr. Bird was very excited.
"It's Junior!" he shouted.
"What a beautiful baby!"

Junior opened his mouth.

It was a big mouth.

It was full of teeth.

"That's the funniest-looking baby
I ever saw," said Mrs. Bird.

"Something is wrong.

I don't think he's our baby at all!"

"He's in our nest, so he must
be ours," said Mr. Bird.
"His mouth is open.
That means he's hungry.
When your baby is hungry,
you feed him."
Mr. and Mrs. Bird went away
to get some food for Junior.

Mr. Bird brought
a pink worm.

Mrs. Bird brought
a green one.

Junior ate both worms
in one gulp.
Then he opened
his mouth wide again.
"We have to get Junior
lots more to eat,"
said Mr. and Mrs. Bird.

Hour after hour, day after day,
they brought food for Junior.

Mrs. Bird got berries and cherries.

She got butterflies and caterpillars.

She got dragonflies and mosquitoes.

She got ladybugs and tiger beetles.

Mr. Bird got crickets and spiders.

He got grasshoppers and snails.

He got red ants.

He got black ants.

He got centipedes, too!

"What kind of bird
eats so much?" said Mrs. Bird.

"It doesn't matter," said Mr. Bird.
"He's still hungry
and we have to feed him."
Weeks went by.
Junior never stopped eating.

And he never...

...stopped growing.

He grew **bigger**...

and **bigger**...

and bigger!

Finally Junior got so big
that Mr. Bird said,
"It's too crowded up here.
Junior has to leave the nest.
It is time for him
to fly away."

"You are right," said Mrs. Bird.
"The time has come.
We must show him
how to fly."

Mrs. Bird pushed
and pushed.

Mr. Bird showed Junior how to fly.

"Jump into the air like this," he said.

"Then flap your wings."

Junior got ready.
He took a big breath
and jumped.
Up...up...up into the air
he went.

"Flap your wings!" yelled Mrs. Bird.

"Flap your wings!" yelled Mr. Bird.

Junior flapped and flapped.

But it didn't do any good.

He didn't have any wings!

Down…down…down went Junior.

Down into the water.

SPLASH!

It was cool and wet in the water.
It was just right for Junior.

"You know," said Mrs. Bird,

"I don't think Junior was a bird at all!"

"It doesn't matter," Mr. Bird said.

"He's happy now.

And just look at him swim!"

August 2003

Maxi & Aidan

<u>Remember</u> when we
read this book for
the first time?
In Boston the first
time you where both
visiting Oma + Opa. We
had a great time. We love you
OMA + OPA